I0769567

# HOME

Bob Fletcher

ISBN 979-8-218-54190-3

Printed with IngramSpark

Portions of this book appeared in HERE, published by Special Collections Press, University of Cincinnati 2018

# Contents

## *POISE*

# HOME

# PRIMER

# Mischief

Now here we are, all genially cracked.
There's the sparrow in her make-shift bath.
Innocence is scuffling down this path.

Underfoot, lost leaves are torn and cracked.
I bent to find my own bewildered eyes.

The sky rose deep within the drum-tight skin
grown by this pond on breezeless days.
My twin, his halo blue and cloudy, found my eyes.

Upon reflection, so predictable!
—except that everything that's right was left.

Then the membrane shuddered and was cleft:
a frog had found a fly delectable.

Some say time's too stingy, late and soon.
And some say life breaks hearts until they stop.

Some say love's a mirror you can drop,
or that you're both the clapper and the tune.

Now the sparrow's song skipped hit and miss.
A raucous croak rasped gravely out of tune.
It seemed tranquility had passed too soon.

This mischief, though, had breached a gate to bliss.
Wave patterns stroked the skin and shook it out.

I waited, waited, till I saw his smile,
and then my finger poked at him awhile,
and then I stood and gave a startled shout.

# Breeze

Perhaps you can remember being three.
a scene from long ago, still there to see.

A bucket full of coals, and, curious,
a square-shaped solid yardstick at your chest,
your brother's pirate voice, faux furious—
to send you off the plank? Then all the rest.
Me sitting in the coals, the screams, the rush
to stop the pain. Flung down. The sudden hush.
The coals and plastic brand, when stripped away,
had stripped me, too, peeled me to the bone.
I lay face down. They had a lot to say.
The car. Must stay awake. Must stand alone.
Yet

       I remember drafts of autumn breeze
       lifting my tee-toweled dress above my knees.

# Fears



Oh!

Oh, it—
it feels like I,

I'm never gonna know—
know the easy feeling,

easy feeling, foolish falling,

fool falling holding all he owns.

We own just what we've loved,
loved through every fear

while my fears mount—
mount so high,

so, so

—high.

# Anglo

He could write a song about being held near a jolly bodice in a velvet
blouse, deepest red, with massive squash blossom necklace and heavy
silver bracelets, black hair in a bun tied round and round with white
string, when he was a baby

or running naked after his mother until the snow and cold drove him
back inside to the coal fire, when he was three

or watching his thirsty grandmother dig at the sand near a cotton-
wood tree on the bottom of Canyon de Chelly, the water pooling up
for her to drink, when he was four

or climbing what was left of an old fence to mount a wild donkey his
brothers were leading, when he was five

or combing the dirt for piñons under the trees on the high plateau,
eager to bite-crack the tender shells and roll out the sweet meat,
when he was six

or helping his father create that enormous garden of irrigated corn,
growing taller than his reach, and harvesting it, and putting it away,
when he was seven

or watching, cold and thrilled, the giant Shalako dancers at night in
the snow, hiding from the torchlights of the pueblo, when he was
eight

or riding Blaze, bareback with a rope halter, through the tangled
mesquite to his water reward at the artesian well, and then the
thigh-gripping, mane-grabbing gallop back home, when he was nine

or tasting book after book, salvaged from the disorderd bricks of a discarded library, by the light of the fireplace, on the Two Gray Hills rug, when he was ten

or climbing the hogbacks day after day, deeper and deeper, exploring cavecracks and hidden mesas, building hollow tumbleweed shade in dented draws, when he was eleven

or finding, in the midst of a high forest of ponderosas, a callow grove of aspen, white trunks and bruised knees like mine, crayola leaves dancing with the breeze, when he was young.

Soon enough they moved near a town, where he was an Anglo.

# Gates

When the bell rings for the new day's first class,
    she's caught standing knee high in piles of books in
        paths of snow the students find the door.
            Mother's loosing the chains that held us out within
                our stone house there is age and mass.
                    Ancient dust webs the panes and trails from hooks near
                        fresh laid beds, frayed rugs relieve the floor.
We harvest loss, parched by a sea like glass on         She shares, she bears our cares, within and out.
    a raw desert beach. She overlooks.
        Ruin dissolves bluffs to chasms we ignore in
            a tumbleweed reel we rock and shout.
                Our whims compose cacaphonies of sass with
                    measures spun by friends. We hurl the books.
                      We reach through gates. We desecrate our shore for
When the bell rings                       the glory, but reach the drifts of doubt.
    she's caught standing knee high in
        paths of snow
            Mother's loosing the chains in
                that stone house
                    ancient dust webs the panes near
                      fresh laid beds
                        she shares, she bears our cares.

We harvest loss on
    a raw desert beach
        ruin dissolves bluffs to
            a tumbleweed reel
                our whims compose with
                    measures spun by friends
                        we reach through gates for
                            the glory. We reach.

When caught in
    chains,
        stone webs of
            fresh cares,
                harvest raw ruin with
                    tumbleweed whims.
                        Spin through gates for
                            glory. Reach.

Caught in cares,
    harvest whims,
        spinning through gates
            of glory.


Reach.

# Brother's Duet

She's got a bag of hammers here
to beat upon her heart.
She's in a country western tune;
I've got to play my part.
    *When I say I love you,*

            *belly laugh,*
    *and kiss the one beside you*
    *then tell me when it's over*
    *you'll settle down and be my better half.*

Now how does she believe my tale
of just one time one night,
when everyone around here knows
I took a bigger bite?
    *When I say it hurts me,*

            *shake your head,*
    *then tell me to forget it*
    *and warn me if I love you*
    *I'll think of all our happy times instead.*

She's got a bag of hammers here.
She'll grab the one she likes.
She'll grip it hard and swing it high
when I hand her the spike.
    *When you smile at me, please,*

            *don't explain,*
    *just warn me I'm not blameless*
    *that you've become so shameless*
    *though you get all the pleasure from our pain.*

***There's that mirror on our wall***
    ***where shadows swing and swear***
***before they fall.***

She found my clothes thrown on our bed.
I'd changed and let them drop.
She laid them out to look like me.
She wondered when I'd stop.
>    *When we hear the knocking,*
>                        *later on,*
>    *just chat inside the doorway,*
>    *later meet up in the foothills,*
>    *while I act like I'm careless if you're gone.*

She's got a bag of hammers here.
She'll carry it awhile,
and when the kids arc grown and gone
she'll hit herself and smile.
>    *When I chased your lies down*
>                        *to the street,*
>    *the one I saw you kiss,*
>    *too late at night to miss,*
>    *just chuckled with delight at your deceit.*

She wondered why I never cared
the crowd would see my play,
but her despairing heart—
it clapped the loudest, in its way.
>    *When you choose to settle*
>                        *your affairs,*
>    *just keep me at arm's length*
>    *and clean and paint the place,*
>    *till you've decided time has made repairs.*

**Do the children have to see**
         **hearts broken all apart**
**before they're free?**

She's got a bag of hammers here
so we can break her heart.
She wouldn't want to make me fear
she hasn't learned her part.
   *When we lie together*

         *in the night,*
    *you clasp my hand and whisper,*
    *—It was never better, ever—*
    *while I just lie there waiting for the light.*


*That's quite a bag a hammers, dear,*
*but we've got worlds of time.*
*Let's just aim to keep the beat.*
*Somehow we'll force our rhyme.*


*That's quite a bag a hammers, dear,*
*and love's too plain to miss.*
*Let's just aim to keep the beat,*
*and swing with every kiss.*

# Old Homes



Old homes of stucco, brick, and wood,
and stone and stone and stone,
suburban cracker box, suburban moan,
country cabin, citified, but then the backyard flat,
      I moved from one to other
       till I had enough of that.

Old homes with hollow laughter, prayers,
and fights and fights and fights,
worship till it hurts and tithing bites,
country school and Sunday School and every scolding palm.
      I reeled from one to other
       till I stole away some calm.

Old homes that burned black coal or wood,
and cold and cold and cold,
dust beating at the panes until we sold,
the flues and doors and windows rocking, shaking tambourines.
      I strayed into a meadow,
       and gleaned what silence means.

Old homes, I've found a few of you,
remembered you were mine.
Some were pulled apart as if a sign.
Falling all to pieces, losing all our leases,
yet it seems just yesterday
      I slipped away.

# Dream

Fond days and luscious nights and sweetest dreams,
      dreams to remember, not forget,
the mind at rest unknitting clotted seams,
      needlepointed cares, to let
the spirit drape at ease. Well, at its best
      that's the way it ought to be.
My dreams so seldom pass this test,
      stitching scraps of thought debris,
of ragged bonds, rough words, and unkempt moods
      into crazyquilts, while reason broods.

I have a dream of falling from a car,
      four years old, forgotten, loose.
I dream of seeking shelter, somewhere far
      under and away, abstruse.
I dream of flying, using arms for wings,
      tangling in the power wires.
I dream I sing a psalm so sweet it brings
      tears to eyes, sating desires.
I dream of running with unending breath,
      deft without a thought of death.

Then I wake. I stitch my day together,
      seeking order whatever comes,
trying to ensure my in and outer weather
      balance the books with matching sums.
Dreams can last the night and be discarded.
      Dreams may last but a beat of the heart.
Dreams can dye the day if left unguarded,
      walk the stage without a part.
Logic and its cousins may dissemble.
      Visitations make me tremble.

I do not sleep to dream, nor dream to rest.
        I sleep, and I forget. In sleep I find
that I am blessed, so often, with a guest
        that knows the smallest sights my mind declined
to hold, and leads me by oblique
        and winding indirection anywhere
its random will proceeds. I sneak a peek
        at things I never knew, not half aware
if I'm to blame nor what's ahead, nor how
        to turn the page and recollect my now.

Precious, oh, so precious, turns of mind,
        finding other ways when I am blind.

# Notes of A Mild Man

Drinking causes big blunders.
Sobriety is safest.
Never lose track of yourself.

Anger should remain be a private matter.
Even if you show it, you don't need to discuss it.
Let sleeping dogs lie.

It is honorable to be poor.
Wealthy people usually have dark sides.
Don't accumulate what you can't live without.

The simplest people are the most genuine.
The oddest people are the most sincere.
Be as proud as you want of your humility.

Finding a lot in common with others makes a smooth operator.
Take care to be yourself, but don't stand out too much.
Don't get too big for your britches.

Experts usually know just one thing well.
Asking for advice doesn't mean you'll take it.
Don't let anyone tell you what to do.

Education has a high value.
Highly educated people are often the biggest fools.
Don't trust too much in what you know.

The best art is familiar; anyone can see that.
Don't bother with the far out, but only with what strikes home.
Beauty doesn't need much reflection.

Acting sensibly requires using your instinct.
Trusting your instinct requires a lot of reflection.
Nobody really knows for sure what's going on.

Trust the ones closest to you,
Put distance between you and those mistaken.
Moving often demonstrates balance and flexibility.

Moving helps you negotiate community.
Living with others requires private spaces.
A place deep in the country is most ideal.

When the family gets together, find a quiet place to think.
When the family is apart, savor the quiet time.
Anticipate company, but rejoice in your own.

Walking to the light means coming from darkness.
Darkness closes every day.
Get up early.

# Bread

The doorbell never worked.
You had to pound to get an answer, shout till you were found.
That's if you made it past the empty hook next to the gate.
Something used to swing there. Wasn't now.
Ignore the time it took to bud and blow
and leave the leaves each spring.
Neglected bushes slapping at your face.
What made her pay the price to claim this place?
She could have a high desert shack.
The wind would scour her windows clean.
But some poor souls might stumble on her track
through the sand or snow and bust her whole routine.

> Well, you can't make them love you if they don't.
> They can't make you love them if you won't.
> Might be they'd scout the kitchen first.
> Ice, or boil the water? Both.
> They'd cruise the art stuck on the icebox,
> cheap at any price.
> The cushions. Pile them.
> Wait. Spread them apart.
> Neighbors, maybe?
> Flushed with some complaint?
> It might just be a pilgrim.
> Or a saint.

Stranger, brother, mother, friend, or dad?
That lock just serves to sanctify your key.
No telling if it's good or if it's bad,
All is only what you help it be.

> The bread is sliced, the knife's aside.
> Begin.
> Pour a glass of wine.

Time to let us in.

# Folly

If you find the fairest way to speak,
must there be no melody to play?
if you take the time to find your seat,
should the ticket be for anywhere?

Must I answer why I made the song;
must I miss some notes and bow it wrong.
Should I hold my breath until I'm done;
should I have to wonder why you care.

The mind can be an instrument to lose.
The heart can be a cataract that soothes.
You find your way by making something up.
I drink my deepest from your broken cup.

If time should come for me to wave hello
because you've said goodbye to what you know,
you might break a rule upon a dare.
You might own a smile that I could wear.

The folly of the plain
is that there's none.
The folly of the free
is there's but one.
There's folly if your pattern isn't true.
The folly of the faultless
won't find me.

# Play

My students come to me to say
they'd like to have me watch them play.
Perhaps there's something I can learn
that they can't teach me if I stay.

They sense that I won't be so stern
when quarrels rise or tempers turn
if sun's above and grass below
and only laughter's left to earn.

I walk among them just to show
I used to be a kid and know
a bit about the job of fun,
although it changes as you grow.

They play together in the sun.
I help them through who's lost and won
while they teach me just how it's done.
They always teach me how it's done.

# Fallen Leaf
for Jesse

Outside the door they pin a fallen leaf
to let one know that here a newborn died.
The nurses enter and attend to grief.

The birth itself brings something like relief,
since he has gone, gone days before he cried.
Before her time, they've pinned a fallen leaf.

Before he cried, she cries, we cry. The thief
has found him in the safest place to hide.
We celebrate by tending to our grief.

It often seems the time we share is brief.
We bless ourselves and humbly say, I tried.
We feel the wind, then pin our fallen leaf

on our own door. We're nursemaids for the thief.
This child came to us. Certainly he died.
Eternity, I think, most honors grief.

So place him in forever, make him Chief,
and spend each moment always by his side.
On every door we'll pin a fallen leaf,
and every instant celebrate our grief.

# Koya-san

Jostling through the crypts,
shadows throng the forest paths
coursing Koya-san.

Red-bibbed stone infants
tilting through the weight of years
stir with our hushed breath.

Each moment's secret
whispering past, glimpsed pressing
back into the stones.

Compassion's kisses
bound in every broken heart
playing hide and seek.

# Summer



Soft footfalls in the needles; twine-bound sheaves
hand-stacked by threes to dry; old gloves; short sleeves;
and welcome sweat from grappling each bright day
with wayward twigs on paths in cobbled shade
to beaches sentried by madrone,
past hay awaiting binder, thresher, baling blade.
Dawn, nesting owls stand guard.
Noon, hawks hunt high.
At dusk, above my barn bed, bats burst by.
We've planned and prayed and planted, courting fates.
Our garden's trusting the divine design.
All's swollen, readied, ripe, and harvest waits:
the bread; the feast; the nuptials; and the wine.
Children gather. Laughter gathers.
Light and breathing deepen,
lasting longer.
All is right.

# *PINIONS*

# Master of Disgrace



I've walked this way so many times, my feet
just move themselves. My eyes take in the street;
there's nothing to surprise me. Till I fall.
I swear I see my ass pass by in front,
most languidly, as all my boxes sprawl,
and I, arms flying, pinwheel through my stunt.
I've landed just in back of my left knee.
Long pause, Exactly where it ought to be.
I glance around. I try to build a face
That claims control. A master of disgrace,
my dignity demands I claim this dance.
--I meant to do that. [picking up each box]
Nothing's broken. Had to take the chance.
We're all just fine. I'll just pull up my socks.—
But for a while there, spinning through the air,
You would have thought God had me by the hair.

# Hard Weather

He never savored the gritty taste of sand
nor ever favored abruptly frozen mud.
They told him just to join in with the band.
They told him just to sidestep any blood.

He'd try to run through the blinding hip-high snow
or dodge a sun so damned bright the dirt would dance.
They thought his holey socks were just for show.
They thought his stammered steps tracked the main chance.

Flushed with grace,
twisty smile on his face,
holes in his soles
and left in the light,
right in hard weather.

# The Teacher

Lois taught school children off and on through the years, usually fifth graders. She spent a lot of time dealing with the fifth grader in all of us. Sometimes it seemed she was a teacher in spite of herself. If someone didn't know something, Lois was there to teach, no matter her level of expertise. I was by no means her finest student. What Lois taught me is not always what I learned, and there were consequences.

She was confident that she spoiled her children. She let us know that we'd been given everything we needed; it wasn't about us, and the world didn't owe us a living. Rather, we owe a debt we can never repay. True enough, though not shameful. I try my best not to keep score of blessings, in the give and take of love.

She protected us. We lived in some rough communities, surely bathed in grace but also swept by sin and violence, but Lois wouldn't acknowledge fear. She wanted us to stand up for ourselves, feeling that often the best defense was a good offense because it kept you going forward rather than looking backward. Even anger was energy. Forgiveness was our struggle. What I've learned, what I've had to learn, is to atone for my righteousness, especially by saying: I don't know, I'm sorry, I need help, I was wrong.

She had great fun fishing, even if she didn't catch anything but a good conversation. And so, if I listen to others with an open heart, I must learn something, because everyone has something to teach.

Her care and attention, her sustained focus, were strained in the service of her family of six. She was not a good cook, negligent both to time and taste, with a minimal budget in any event. Tithing on Sunday required squeezing the weekday pennies. She was abstemious, excepting coffee. She dutifully provided meals, rarely fancy, usually sufficient, often slightly singed here or there. Enough was enough.

Our bread's journey, from dough to oven to table, was uncertain. As my appetites grew, I learned to forage.

She liked to tell stories, and improved on them without remorse. When the simplest explanation was not enough, she kept scratching. In even the last retelling there was usually a little truthiness. Regarding the whole garment of Truth, I cling to the scraps I can gather, for modesty's sake.

In the family, you could fool some of the people all the time and all the people some of the time but you couldn't fool Lois, not unless she agreed. She would stand by her man, yet not let him know who was in charge. She attempted many skills with uneven mastery, and had but One Master. I struggle not to fool myself.

She could deliver her observations with dramatic flourish and her opinions with panache. She employed persuasion and invoked unanimity. I was often in the minority, fearing consistency might be a hobgoblin of minds. I have learned that an open, even empty mind can leave gates unlocked to encounter mystery.

By the light of this woman, I've appreciated my blessings—my own children and grandchildren, my own students, my own relationships, the whole world, actually and specifically. I practice, ably or ineptly, the qualities of mercy, even if I'm convinced that I know people better than they know themselves. Sometimes I give them a praising for their own good, just for the glory of it, whether they thank me for it later or not. I've vowed to keep practicing love for my children without conditions, and for their children, and on, even if children don't hold up their end of the deal.

I learned, with Lois' vagrant enthusiasm, that everyone is special, everyone is above average, every relationship is unique. I also learned well that what saints are among us do not abuse our trust, that faith has its reward, however unexpected.

Lois had a good grip. She held on. Her last lessons were in turning loose. These last many years, many sparrows were not watched. I have learned that wherever you go, there you are, even if it looks different. I'm still learning, and Lois is still teaching, that silence can be golden. After all, she delivered me in Stillwater, and, so it goes: still water runs deep.

# Hollyhock

The Coca-Cola bottle full of bees
was thick and green,
corked with a bloom of hollyhock.
It was obscene

the way they fought against the glass,
the bulbous bloom,
each other, trying to find a way to pass
back into spring.

The crippled dog could never understand
what he should do
to partner his new master at the game.
Around them flew

more bees, perhaps with no intent to harm.
Both boy and dog
jumped and bumped each other in alarm.
A shout and bark!

He nearly dropped it. Kicked the dog away.
Secured the plug
and held the bottle high against the sun,
knowing, and smug.

But something felt all wrong. Not just the bees.
He heard the dog,
the whimpers as it cringed against his knees,
confused and hurt.

That's when the evil fell away and left
these two alone.
The boy knew what it felt like when the world

did not atone.
Some pulse beyond the fur and hands took place—
the eyes, the face—
some sapiential sight was rearranged,
exchanged. All changed.

He pulled the cork and let the bees escape.
He apologized.
He soothed the injured limb. He bent to drape
dismay with trust.

The dog invoked his conscience to the last.
The boy might fail, but when he let his friend
sit at the bench, the judgement, sure and fast,
was mercy, and compassion, to the end.

# Bass

My fish, my little mountain trout, were always dead before I ate them. They were dead before I cleaned and cooked them. They'd never seen the sea, and didn't see much of me.

My first time at sea, I remember the friend of my new father cleaning fish. Red hair above a smile, bright red face. The sea bass in a bucket on the dock, waiting for the sacrifice.

Scotty sold tires, in the arid inland flats over the mountains. But he had a boat and friends and loved to fish. So tonight we'd dine al fresco on a floating dock, a wooden island in the sea.

The fish were not as pleased as Scotty. Live and fresh, patient or protesting, panting in a pail's slight pool. Not quite out of water, unable to center upright, without the room inside or out to do the things that mattered. They didn't understand.

Now Scotty—here's the thing—he cleaned them live to keep them fresh. Carved each one open, spread it flapping, flapping in torment, reached in, grabbed and pulled. He washed the first one in the bucket watching me.

Is that the way you do it here, Scotty? Scotty? Scotty knew. He knew what I meant. It's okay, he told me, they're dying anyway. Picked up the next one, flapping, flapping, rolled it belly up and panting. They don't feel a thing. Spilled its belly.

My heart began a wild flapping, flapping, angry and lonely. And I felt the ocean rise up in me and pour out over every thing there was. I tried to swim in my salt water and center myself, patient, protesting, panting, panting. But I couldn't save my innocence.

Red hair above a smile, bright red face. Red heart, red hearth. Eat hearty. God in heaven. Gods in heaven. Hear our prayers, now and in these hours.

# Bites

My,
my, my.
Maybe why
words,
small for use,
ate
a captive goose,
    *a fowl that turned them loose,*
        *loose to warm the self and soul,*
            *but overreaching, slipped control,*
                *strutting past the farmer's idle blade*
                    *where saucy prayers lie heavy on the preyed,*
is that our shelter should reflect on what it shades.

# Appetites

I don't really know why you are here.
The lesson for today's not awfully clear.
I can't assemble anything I dream
or locate half the parts.

Just add some salt to savor,
sweeten just before you steam.
Pray appetites forgive the baker's faults.
We can't live on bread alone.

We crave liquor's license, buttered lamb. We're brave!
Haggis, okra, liver, eggs and wombs,
cactus ferment, fungi, grasses, weeds!

We throw it down and march on
      to the tomb.
Smoke, drugs, bugs!
      And anything that bleeds.
Such dishes that we set before our souls.
      The wishes that won't fill my beggar's bowl.

# Perhaps



When I am far away or left behind
and nothing will sustain what I've opined,
when everything has added one more leaf
to what had been a sprawled, unfinished book
parsed ruthlessly by feigning disbelief,
my finger tracing shadows as it shook,
it may be that the echo I will hear
is the sound of answers prowling near,
the bright and hungry predators of faith
with essay questions roiling in their tracts,
wide maws of helpful hints, a fetid wraith
of true and false listing brashly from their backs,
as everything that closes off escape
assumes at last a feral famished shape.

# Medina

I followed scents induced by time's bazaars,
untried and rare, with pride in random scars
rendered to myself in my attempt
to find my way through old medina deeps.
Brushing past raw braziers of contempt
I bargained for the secrets silence keeps.
Seen: hanging drapes above a dyer's drum,
costume-shades of who I might become.
I often missed the open hand of grace
thrust into light, hiding in plain sight,
while I explored the novel in each face
and had my pockets picked of my birthright,
still seeking answers from a stranger's tongue,
distracted by the shadows dreams had flung.

# Spring One



These goddamn birds just have to say
the same things every goddamn day.
It's a crying shame.
Why can't they play in someone else's ears
and stay away from here?
They seem designed
as acoustic feathered, flocking engineers
intent on mocking any peace I find.
They're blocking reveries of grave compassion,
with trills and squawks of flighty wiredrawn passion.
I love this island's dawn,
the glowing rose throws stain upon the sea and cloud-strewn sky.
Then on my ears, past rhythmic surf, there grows
the bedlam chorus tuning up on high.
Please, Lord, this spring: one moment's peace is all.
I'll try to love the birds before the fall.

# Rains

The rains came down today.
Heavy showers.
But I still hear the birds above.
Not one cowers.
Three birds are busy hunting through the grass.
A bird just there above my chair is singing
like a piper in the company of brass—
the peal of flattened leaves,
pelted, ringing.
His four note call I've come to know has grown
more complicated,
syncopated,
jazz blown.
Spontaneous and free, such innocence
makes me jealous.
I'm stuck inside.
What keeps me here?
Is longer life a recompense?
I want to fly, not make my little leaps.
Nothing keeps me down but god alone.
Or fate.
I'll sing! and turn them into stone.

# Fall

Momentum lent my temper bullish grace.
Again against assurances my face
contorted to a frozen slide
until what thoughts humility or love might broach
could not withstand the slope
but rolled downhill,
crescendoing in stammer,
their approach a chastened, chastening rebuke.
You sighed and braced yourself;
you took the blow and cried.
Between us like a veil you shed your tears.
Experience belied the simple hymns exhaustion wove
while softly folding fears
of ruined, eroded love
in quaking limbs.
Still, outside:
mottled midday leaves,
whose fall is not forever,
scolding as they sprawl.

# Winter



Beside her as she listens fold her hands.
Her casual precision reprimands
the lines—
of vacant hospitality he prates and calibrates,
of blinded light
whose slanting scales score flat banality—
with elusive nods of thoughtful oversight.
While bracing her to implicate his worth,
his gravely fluttering finger taps her mirth.
Composed in this suspension, she refrains,
reflective. Muted strains, diffusive airs,
distract their staid repose;
reserve profanes the balance of their languid jibing.
Prayers, she measures, passage barred,
may harbor in keys of graceful poise,
yet scatter harmony.

# Duck



It was quiet by the pond until the duck quacked.
The peacefulness of dawn had had its deep cracked.
Falling down means falling up is what the priests say.
Frailty is strength when I hear blues play.

Will there be a sweet release when I have lost?
Laughter at my prize and what it cost?
Time will tell, unless I lose my place.
My empty hands will yield one last embrace.

# Blues

If your days seem old
and the beds are cold
and the sun doesn't shine on your stroll,
you can trust the blues
to bring the news
that a leaf in the wind finds you droll.

Scratch some answers with a twig,
render tears just like the flood,
conceit makes castle keeps from sand,
with palette plates to paint the mud.

If there be some mild misunderstanding,
let there be some solace in our folly.
May the blessings of the deep confound us.
May the limpid blues sound almost jolly.

If your days seem old
and the beds are cold
and the sun doesn't shine in your soul,
you can trust the blues
to bring the news
that the stars still find you droll.

# Gambol

Carnality compiles a list
of what it knows and what it's missed.
It urges us to secret strange,
and cocks its head when choices change.

If purses packed with Billys do
are promises we must pursue,
we muscle up before the start
with thickened blood and thudding heart.

Then whether chisel splits the rock
or master key turns in the lock
or birds are startled off the line,
a table's laid with figs and wine.

Some satisfaction still remains
after all the pleasure drains.
      Our risk must be its own reward,
      when love is all we can afford.

# Anchor

I have an anchor in my heart
that keeps me holding fast if my night watchman sleeps.
Sometimes it slips, when dreams are rough, unkempt,
tossing the deeps against the straining line
dropped in comfort's cove.
My heart's attempt to keep its place
must alter its design.
The deeps announce their power to displace
the architecture of complacent grace.
So all the shadowed depths may shrug
beneath my craft of handmade expertise,
and leave me feeling quite at sea.
I hug the deck,

an amateur upon my knees.
Some nights it seems the compass spins around.

Then I must wake.
Then I must walk the ground.

# Coals



This fire might go out any time.
It flickers and it smokes.
A remnant of my heat will climb up through the narrow way.
The sight evokes burnt offering, the grace I hope to coax.

Today began to weep and whine.
I've countered with the flames to salvage just a little shine.
Should I build a pyre of faults
that claims to sacrifice, for paradise, my shames?

If so, this blaze might never ease.
Here's a chair to rest. This practice sent me to my knees.
I'll confess I'm stingy even blessed,
and hoard my fortune like my soul's possessed.

The fire's so low. I need more sin.
I should have flailed and failed with tougher skin, a haughty grin,
and piled the booty higher while they bailed,
but no, but no, but no, that ship has sailed.

Patience, and the oak will burn, if coals would ever form.
Regret would smolder to a turn.
I'll toss an unearned blessing to stay warm
and rue my loss of virtue to the storm.

The unentitled windfall that I choose
is laughter in the night when there's everything to lose:
we carved such dreams of hope and flight
we wept while doubled over by the sight.

It's hot and high now! noxious, too, a sacrament of hell,
but I'm still grateful, lord, to you.
I'm old and tired, but still aware and well, forgiven and debt-free,
till I rebel again.

# Wings

Inconstant understanding, hold my hand a bit.
I've organized my day around our tete a tete.
I've gathered what I know to calculate my bet,
       but all the odds are stacked against the hairs I've split.

This game just waits for players. The gold returns to dust.
We measure up and down to pass another test.
We're brazen on the baize. We bluff with all the rest.
       Our gambol green ensures that all the hearts go bust.

At night we cripple home, unsanctified and broke.
The things we could have done with any sort of breaks.
We had it all but then they always raised the stakes!
       Damn everything we heard and every word we spoke.

I'd cheat, I'd cheat if cheating's not the same as wrong.
I'd make a copy, every key left on her ring.
I'd need to find the lock that unlocks everything.
       Unlock the spring, unfar the star, unend the song.

Then feathers, jesus, feathers. Feathers on your chest.
Push off and go, just fly! Or float. You'd be a beast
if you had wings. I'd be a hummingbird at least.
       If I could still be me, but fly, I'd settle for the rest.

You'll have to preen, if you're a bird, to zip your feathers tight.
You'll have to learn a cry, and not because of fate.
You'll need their common voice to join their great debate,
       or just to get a date, or find her in the night.

We need to laugh. That's in the heart of it. Can they?
They'll chuckle, scold, and woo, enjoy the dawn, But laugh?
        I've heard their mocking gibes, pitched on my behalf.
        Heard blues turn into folly, spied them at their play.

        Enough. They could be me. I need to learn to fly.
Inconstant understanding, if you would be so kind,
if I can still be me, and fly, and you don't change my mind,
let's keep it light, sing songs all day, feathers fanned and fine.

Just wing it like we planned and tuned it, to that grand design.
        Watch out for hawks.
        And laugh.
        And every body cry.

# Finch

In a small town in New Mexico on Route 66, in its only high school, which caught in its dragnet students from new and ancient families far and near, there was a fight. There were always fights at school, but this one left a trail of blood in the hall to the boys' bathroom. Probably a knife involved, so a serious fight.

It happened occasionally with the boys. It might have been some Anglo, a white kid. They mostly used belt buckles and pointy-toed cowboy boots, against anybody really. They could blow if someone looked them in the eye.

It might have been a Spanish guy, New Mexican Spanish, proud, Cantor born and bred, against a fellow from somewhere south of the border, Mexico, or maybe further south.

Or it might have been an Indian with a blue lunch ticket against a Navajo, Diné, in from the dormitory. Those feelings could get bitter. Blue tickets meant a world of difference. Indians with blue tickets for their cheap hot lunch, Johnson O'Malleys, went home at night. They weren't from the reservation like the dormitory Diné. No one was allowed freedom from the dormitory, so the only place to fight an outlier was at school.

Anyway, it was tough to tell whose blood tracked through the hallway. Could be anyone's.

William Finch was just gathering himself after Julius Caesar, spinning from heights of sarcasm and betrayal, regret and naked insight, meaning Mark Antony in high English, and then shaking back into reality. Straightening his glasses. Searching eyes. Searching the hallway riot of passing bodies in shades of white and brown, Indian and Spanish, spinning gears to dance into that hallway. He seemed out of place, out of step. Everything about him appeared short. His body was just too short for his actual round face, his hair was cut burr short, short sleeves. No one wore short sleeves unless they were rich and anglo and arrogant about it, and this boy was clearly not rich. It was his shoes that told that tale. They were not rich shoes but soft hush puppies that would never manage the weather and be the same, the sand and rocks, mud and snow. Then his skin. Was that freckles or acne? It was both. Lots of spots around his, not a smile, a scared rictus of sham confidence.

William Finch braced himself, then square-shouldered out of the classroom in a military fashion, by planting his left foot and pivoting quickly, self consciously, ninety degrees to the right, brushing down the wall, marching to a corner. Another planted left, another accented pivot, marching off, disappearing into the bodies of Cantor High. A new kid, soldiering off to a fresh battle in a strange arena.

Thomas had noticed William. Their English classes faced each other and they walked out of class at each other. Thomas was almost always last to leave English, school books carefully balanced on his large notebook and gripped tightly under his arm, His hair was deftly waxed into shape. Even though he was, to be sure, lower middle class, he changed his shirt every day, looked put together, kept his nose clean. He was all about control and grades and student government and world peace, even if he had to cheat, and, since he'd already given himself permission, he did cheat, even when it wasn't strictly necessary. And though Thomas was proud, he was wisely discreet, being spare in testosterone, younger by a year than his classmates. He had learned to trade on a look of casual innocence.

Time had recently given Thomas enough serenity to practice empathy safely, when he noticed his shadow across the busy hallway. A boy very much as he saw himself in his worries, another Thomas, seemingly arrogant, an outlier, too, but now too obviously undone. And also small. Small in stature, yes, but also small in pride, in joy, feigning indifference. Courage on trial.

The fight managed to shake William Finch up. A mob of boys were suddenly racing toward him. Should he keep going or turn around, run with them or away from them, surrounded? He didn't know or trust a soul among them, so:  the enemy chasing you is probably my friend. He just kept marching to class, hugging the wall, right toward the trouble. It was a good instinct. The boys clattered by, and now he could see the bloody shoe prints chasing under them, right past his classroom door. Stepping over the blood and into the classroom, it was like sand had flown into his eyes; he couldn't see his way clearly. Nearly doubled over scared, bent over his little blessings, his skin color, the safety of his desk. Sitting down, safe, bent over his books, tapping his pocket with the lunch money, then feeling his relief begin to dry up and wither. He could almost rock with loneliness. He was going to have to learn to deal with this crap, this daily dogfight, and learn quickly. All those kids running past him but then: not a word. No one to talk to, to tell him what happened. No school announcement. Stamp out the fire, fling sand to cover it, rub it in, play on.

Thomas was finally growing familiar with his own fresh set of daily humiliations, now shared with twelve hundred students gathered from the town and the country miles around Cantor High School. He had lived here and there on the reservation for more than a decade, usually the only anglo in his classrooms, counting six, seven, eight different homes before Cantor. And, including all the fractions, a little less than one friend.

Stone homes, wood framed, a cabin, a shack, but now a stuccoed cracker box tract home almost in town, in the middle of a whole hive of anglos who did their best, inadvertently, to educate him in anglo ways and mores. Such as how to survive a day without a fight, something his brothers couldn't grasp. They had found themselves instead as Stompers, named for their boots and their bias and their outsize belt buckles. Strength in numbers.

His parents were adapting to their new town jobs in the Bureau of Indian Affairs relocation program and the schools on the Spanish side of the tracks. Until now they had enjoyed his unconscious forbearance regarding the phantom relatives, dentists, birthday parties, play dates, allowance, even central heating and electric lights. He had, however, taken matters in hand and freely stolen and lied his way to rough parity, save for professional care or spiritual guidance and the like, which he had picked up on the fly, in extremity. Concentrating on public libraries and candy racks, he took what he wanted when he could. He was not above spare change. He was flexible in situations and morals, an equal opportunity player, most comfortable expecting the strange.

It was actually barely a fight. The one good punch was thrown after the bloody toe. Harry the Greek, whose path was often near the edge, had sparked a little contest with an ordinary pocket knife. Carlos Abeyta and Gad Benally stood a few feet apart, standing on the wooden cover for plumbing in the back schoolyard, taking their turns to throw and stick that knife as close to the other's foot as possible. Great fun, inevitable ending, which just delighted Harry. He goaded Gad, who was carefully pulling the knife out of his shoe and dropping it to examine the puncture, to exact his payback. Gad had to lunge to use his fist, because, after all, his toe hurt, blood seeping pretty steadily out of his shoe, but he still managed to hit Carlos a good one on his throat and that was pretty much that, except for the cleanup in the bathroom. Everyone wanted to see what the toe looked like, even Carlos, but, actually, it wasn't that bad. During the turmoil and gimpy run to the bathroom the knife seemed to have just disappeared, along with any coherent account of events, should any authority ask any one.

William sat at his desk, in an air pocket, suspended, echoes of Shakespeare rattling around, through class, through lunchtime, on the bus home, waiting, for nothing.

Thomas had become half good with new acquaintances, always hoping for an actual stand-alone friend, of course, and coming close a few times. Thomas watched William, set out to fix him up, and probably to fix himself a little. Thomas stalked William, but casually.

Followed him in the hallway:

What's your next class?

Do you ride the bus?

Thomas found him in the lunchroom;

Do you want my milk?

I'm never going to own a Ford.

Thomas watched the clouds with him outside;

There's a guy in my church who's a pilot.

I got paddled in seventh grade.

And Thomas asked about his circumstances;

Are you going to the science fair next week?

Have you ever been to Oklahoma?

Thomas learned a little and guessed a whole lot. William Finch was living on the very edge of possible, the other end of town, out past Camerco, about eight or ten miles over in forever flats of tumbleweed. Past anywhere but two straggling bars nearly side by side, an old motel, some isolated trailers busy rusting. Nothing much. Fences to keep out tumbleweeds.

Thomas wondered if William lived in one of those trailers. That would be just like William's father, to stash William in a trailer so he could honeymoon with his new wife. What happened to William's real mother? What happened to his life? Leave him there with some money to budget. Three or four weeks. Catch or miss the school bus into town for the long, rambling weekday circuit. Breakfast? At least lunch, if that was in the budget. And then the long afternoons, and then the dark nights. Cans and crackers in the cabinet. They didn't have television out that far, so a radio. A lot of "I Fall to Pieces" by Miss Patsy Cline. A radio at most. Whatever treat of food or book he'd put by. Maybe a record player! Maybe. And the weekends, the long whole days. Didn't know his neighbors. Didn't have a church.

Thomas feeling, Christ in a bucket. Or somewhere. Not in the Church of Christ. Not the Southern Baptist Church, Catholic cathedral, Mormon tabernacle. Not so much, not right now. Maybe Christ was on a honeymoon. There were churches with no Christ at all, the just God places, a temple, a mosque, a, what's it, ashram. Sweat lodge. A kiva, down in the earth. Waiting for light. Places for dark things, too. Bats. Or birds, but birds in the low light, dusk or dawn, in the air. Just taking flight, that sudden sound that lifts your eyes. Little stitch-

es, little notes free flying across the blue open wide. That deep sky.
Anyway.

Julius Caesar was closer to William than Jesus Christ, even in an
old English play in elevated language, for kids with accents of New
Mexican Spanish, Diné, Hopi, Zuni, cowboy southern, to name
a few, as they struggled to wring out bits of meaning, twisting in
their chairs. It made some sense to William. The tone of self-mock-
ing:
>  *For Brutus is an honourable man;*
>  *So are they all, all honourable men—*
Still he floundered. The false chords, the jangle in his heart:  He
bleeds, yet nothing happened. He loves me; he loves me not. White,
whiter than snow. Washed in the blood.

Thomas generally, genially pried him open a little with an aimless
conversational screwdriver:
>  How do you like English?
>  Are you doing the oration?
And then one day, in the most natural voice, William recited
Mark Antony's funeral oration from memory and Thomas under-
stood every single word. Every single word but on the most meander-
ing, curious line, like watching a woman weave, or more like pouring
different colors of heavy chemicals into a bowl of fluid in a lab, and
watching the colors be themselves for a while, and then mix a little
over here, and then a new color start to braid and blend, and Thomas
had to look away for a second so he could just lose his eyes and use
his mind and his heart. It was like William was teaching him his
mother tongue by direct transference, by some intimate pathway you
weren't supposed to put your fingers on or try to mind map, saying a
song that wielded years of grace notes, of inflections and inferences,
sarcasm and despair, remorse and false virtue, to unerringly contain
but one single tone. A mellow, matter of fact crie de coeur.
Thomas asked to hear it again. William complied. And once again
Thomas understood every single turn in the road and had a pretty

good idea how to get home by following his own nose. That is to say, Thomas understood the oration about as well as he could for a fourteen year old boy with a life left to learn.

That night Thomas read the oration over and again, and invested it with meaning, recalling William's covert, almost whispered, public speech, his compression of force into meaning, his profound dismay framed with knowing composure. Pretty soon, without grave intent, Thomas had put this covenant in his ark. After that, every time he shook it out, spoke it aloud, it unfolded differently, came alive with new invention, like magic, almost like a sacred text.

Soon, on a weekend, the state science fair would be held in Albuquerque. Thomas could hitch a ride on the bus that was taking the students showing projects, but then he was on his own. He'd need to spend the night at Martin's Motel near the UNM campus, which was no problem. He always had some money. He'd graduated from delivering papers on a bike to delivering on a used Lambretta, until now he was using his scooter to commute all the way to his work at Ray's Supermarket. He could pay for the night, and more. He'd need a ride back. He figured that if he got there, well then, he could figure out how to get back, Greyhound bus if he had to. Something. He'd solve that problem when he came to it.

Maybe William would like to come along:

It'll be an adventure!

William nodded:

Sure.

And there the matter rested:

See you Saturday morning.

But Thomas never heard any excitement, questions about who was going and what would happen. There was no talk of what to bring, like clothes or money. No mention of exactly where and when to meet before getting on the school bus. No real discussion about where they'd stay or when they'd be back or how they'd get back. None of that. No friends sharing anticipation.

And no William on Saturday morning, no William on the bus. Since Thomas wouldn't allow himself to expect more than whatever he had, he was more curious than disappointed. Maybe William couldn't get to school, or his folks came home early, or he didn't have the money. Something logistical may have happened. Maybe he had something else planned and didn't want to say, or just changed his mind. That's allowed. No harm done. Didn't matter. It was a thought more than a plan. Still curious, though.

But the fair was not all glory. Even before it began Thomas abruptly got in one almost fight with some local boys pushing ahead in line, shoving young scientists aside. Thomas stood up in righteousness for civility. As the voice of established order, he called a public halt to this anarchy. But, alas, he realized he had miscalculated. The arms of established order did not extend to the crowd outside the auditorium. The door happened to open immediately, and Thomas was sucked into the vast arena. He lost the locals amid the trackless lanes of booths in the huge arena, but caught them following him when he headed outside. He had to hide in the buses until he could run toward Martin's Motel for a lost, languid day of wandering and television.

The following morning, without being trapped by pride or violence, he had better luck, and explored aisles so full of the complicated and curious that he got good and tired of looking and listening to learn. He finally wanted home, and Mr. Springstead, teacher of physical science, wanted to give him a ride.

Thomas succumbed. Thomas was certainly not Springstead's favorite student, but then Springstead didn't have favorite students. He didn't have a wife or family. He lived alone, and all Thomas knew about him was that, hard to imagine, he acted in local plays. Thomas and his family didn't do local plays. Actually Springstead was a little scary when he was almost friendly. Being in the front seat with him, side by side, wouldn't be entirely comfortable for the hours home. Thomas bought a hefty paperback for the miles and had nearly finished it by arrival. Not twenty words passed between them. Thomas was a perfect gentleman and made sure to voice his appreciation for the help. He never saw Mr. Springstead again. It seemed that was true of a bunch of folks.


Bright and lively, like the day itself, Thomas came to school ready to find his friend and ask him what his story was, when, in the bustling hall, a tentative girl tapped Thomas on the shoulder, wondering if he'd heard the news:

What news?

William Finch is dead.

What do you mean, dead?

How do you know?

Are you sure, he's dead?

I heard he shot himself.

That's what you heard.

That's not what you know.

I know he shot himself. With a shotgun. Ask anyone.

Thomas didn't know, for certain sure, what to think. He just felt things, right through his first class. All the while the shadowy rumor kept sliding around. When the bell rang he went to the office. Through the window he could see the principal, Mr Adams, sitting down talking to Mr. Yandell, the vice principal. Mr. Yandell was Thomas's math teacher. Thomas loved his math. Math usually had very clear rules that you needed to follow carefully. Thomas liked having the rules to follow, and if he did, he'd get the right answer. There were always right answers. Thomas worked as hard and honestly and successfully as he could in math, and Mr. Yandell respected him for it; and so he respected Mr. Yandell.

When the secretary said he could go in and ask Mr. Adams a question, both men looked up. It was certainly unusual for Thomas to appear there, and possibly Thomas looked a little urgent around the gills when he walked over to them and looked them up and down.

Mr. Adams raised his head and his eyebrows:

Yes?

Thomas leaned in and over just a little and asked, man to man:

Did William Finch kill himself, with a shotgun?

Mr. Adams closed his face and raised his hand to brush Thomas and his question away, but Mr. Yandell stopped him with a look and said his name:

Bill.

Bill Adams took that in, let it ride. He turned, looked Thomas right in the eye:

Yes, Thomas.

Yes, he did.

He did.

Mr. Yandell nodded. Thomas dropped his eyes to nowhere. Looked out the window. Then he stood up straight, man to man:

Thank you.

That's all I wanted to know.

Thomas turned and walked out, very carefully, away from the men who were waiting for more, past the secretary who was curious. That was not all Thomas wanted to know, certainly. But that's all he ever learned or tried to discover. That was plenty. That was just enough, no more but thank you.


A few weeks later Thomas heard his name over the loudspeaker, asking him to come to the office. He walked past the same secretary who gestured over her shoulder to the principal. But this time there were three men in there: Bill Adams, Mr. Yandell, and an older shorter gentleman in a brown tweed three piece suit such as Thomas had only seen in movies about Scotland or the wild west:

Thomas was introduced to William Finch's father:

This is Thomas.

He was a friend of William's.

I think he can help you find his locker.

William Finch's father was doing his best to assemble an appropriate attitude, switching between mucho gusto to sternly administrative to unavoidably uncertain, when Thomas put out his hand, man to man:

It's good to see you, sir.

Then Thomas turned and led him through the hallway to William Finch's locker, using the words that were necessary, waiting politely at a distance to see if the locker would open, glimpsing some jumbled cords and books and looking down at his shoes as the man slowly reached in, took out a book, let it fall open, sighed, seemed to begin to read. Thomas turned away and went back to class.

Not long after, Mrs. Phillips, who was on Thomas' old paper route and married to a lieutenant colonel from the Fort Kingate armory, had her English students take turns reading from Julius Caesar. Thomas managed to read Mark Antony's funeral oration. He hammed it up, but just a little, and felt almost satisfied with himself:

  The evil that men do lives after them;
  The good is oft interred with their bones.

He must have been a little nervous though, because he felt his throat begin to close before the end.

The next day Mrs. Phillips came over to his desk and asked if Thomas would do her a little favor. She was holding a tape recorder:

  Could you read the funeral oration for me into this recorder?
  I want my husband to be able to hear it.
  You don't have to be loud at all.
  Just right here at your desk.
  You can speak quietly, like you were talking to someone you know.

That's exactly what Thomas did.

# *POISE*

# Domestic Violence

There's a modern invention to preserve freshness.
It's a roll of thin, clear, flexible plastic film you tear off in sheets.
It sticks to almost anything, most stubbornly to itself.
With luck, you can stretch it across a container as a seal.
You must be careful tearing it along the serrated box edge.
The slightest waft will stick it back upon itself, here and there.
My toddler grandson discovered a roll in a cabinet one day.

I watched him carefully unroll yard after yard of it.
It unwound, billowed and snagged, on anything.
Yard after yard, he examined its properties, bemused.
I admired the focus he brought to his calm inquiry.
He could see through it like a twisted lens.
His mother didn't greet the results with his own wrapped joy.
It's very hard to salvage even one taut sheet.

It's like being trapped in mild flirtation with someone too knowing.
The more you struggle, the deeper you're involved.
I wad it up and try again to save my bacon.
No one should ever witness such childish failure.
Just give me one good sheet, godammit.
My wife appears and grasps the situation.
A grab, a rip, and tear, and the bacon's good to go.

Have I ever loved her more?

# Young

Following the creek,
drawn by its shadowed, twinkling flash
and pulsing splash,

I bent to let it lick my cheek.

Something made me shrink.

Sense and instinct made me glance
to see the chance
a buck was taking for a drink.

Cautious eyes, wide, calm,
nose held high, ears shifting quick,
his tail a-flick.

I held my balance with my palm.

Bending down, he seemed
restless, as a doe stepped out
and looked about
and drank, her faith in him redeemed.

Still he held his ground,
braced with caution, poised for flight,
though all seemed right.

Then branches bent without a sound.

From a grove of trees
nearby, an awkward fawn came
to drink the same
water, dare the same enemies.

Pause before the fright.

Sweet peace held us just this while,
enough to smile,
enough to shelter me tonight.

Some dreams, like fawns, should be
made by two, for that's the way
it was today.

And that's the way it shall be with me.

# Nothing

I had a bird and friends gave him a wife.
She nagged him, broke his leg, cost him his life.
I loved him when he wandered up my sleeve,
and loved him when he chortled in my ear.
I loved him when he knew he had to leave.
I told him there was nothing there to fear.
When he was gone, precisely in that space,
nothing moved right in and took his place.
Now I fear nothing seven days a week.
On Sundays I feel nothing's very clear.
No feathers ever brush against my cheek;
no kisses to my ear each time I speak.
My chanted prayers seem lost without a score,
though nothing sings for me outside this door.

# Something Moor



I think this valley's lovely, so serene?
What's this cove called? In Cornish what's that mean?
Oh, see up there, just past those pointy things,
you know, they're sticking up above the trails?
Is that a bird? It's like a kite. Two wings?
It might be hunting. Wait. It's got two tails.
The sun's so bright, you see, the sea and sky?
I always lose my hat; I don't know why.
But look, these flowers are so, you know, red?
Or reddish mauve, or bluish. Stay the same!
The light keeps changing. See that thunderhead?
It might be fog. I never know their names.
The flowers I mean, and cove and cairn, and tor?
Next, after clotted cream, it's Something Moor.

# Aim

The world looked aged with snow.
Rain threatens him today.
He's older, nearly deaf, grown querulous.
His pleasures are in little things, brief, stray.
Banked fires that spark,
sea glow bursting above the road down to the bay.
Most loads seem perilous.
Signs don't always aim at what they say.

Not many of us aim at accident,
but aiming's rarely been his prime intention.
Perhaps the fog would lift,
his shoulder would get tapped.
Meanwhile life requires some invention,
children need attention, plans are scrapped,
a nap becomes a gift,
the days are rarely mapped.

The weather,
raw and rowdy or sultry and unkempt,
retains a space inside for changes to his mood.
He's change itself,
eyesight turning cloudy, seasick with losses.
But as he attempts to glean
from all that's left as tides subside,
there's nothing that he won't include.

Since every day is different from the last
he never needs to act like he's surprised,
while if he'd left a space for every loss
there wouldn't be a place to set his joys.
To find his way across
he flounders past his poise
till every urge has passed
to meet life in disguise.

# Penny

There were no bitter words
to mark the end.
Just didn't want to dark
the door again.

Most wise and high,
your kindness
reached me low,
lower than I felt,
and you more high.

My lines were struck,
redacted to a sigh.
I only wanted free, to go.
Unpin the shadow
I had helped to pen,
take off the costume,
bow, to you,
and leave the stage.
A gentle ending, without tears and rage.
No photograph
to nail the moment in.

After years, at last
the penny dropped,
I took apart the boards and left the land.
Opened up a new house, twice as grand.
Left your ticket at the gate, in case
you stopped.

Our globe is casting plots
that must encompass you and I,
spinning our rehearsals
and reversals,
low to high
or inside out.

All the world's a stage with many parts,
plays opening and closing all the time.
The aisle is full of noises, breaking hearts
to loud applause.

Such changes,
so sublime.

# If

If every lemon tart's been sold to others,
will I have to have the custard with my tea?
If the treadmills of the world all formed a union,
would they let me run in place but raise the fee?
If all the walls have tumbled down around us,
would we cheer because the furniture is free?
> If she sincerely never heard you when you whispered,
> then why are you afraid she'll disagree?

If we do our part precisely does it end there,
or is it wiser just to fumble for the key?
If the wineglass near the crackers stains the mantle,
can you be baptized by a blunder in the sea?
If I meant it at the time but changed it later,
is every choice still possible for me?
> If I sincerely never heard her when she whispered,
> then why do I continue to agree?

Oh, if today the rapture claims us all for heaven,
> will I never have my succulent Bebe?

# Catch

He seems to feel
he needs to heal
the tragedy
of imperfections.

The comedy
of comity,
is dancing to
impromptu questions.

All the grumbling and the stumbling,
all the wiles and all the crying,
all the smiles and all the sighing
distill reflection:

The play's the thing
to catch our king
—but every scene
springs from the king's suggestion.

# Recipes

Enough of that.
Shake off the dust.
Fading notes still season
scents and sense
past reason.
Bitterroot
to leaven trust.

So many times I've cooked my goose.
Salt
refines the taste.
Grief's
too dear to waste.
Clots of rue
release their juice.

Torn crusts will soon be
in the bin.
Knives
replaced and ready.
Fires
banked and steady.
Raise a glass to sin.
      Recipes to save my skin.

# Once

Pushing the wave doesn't turn the tide,
but it turns and returns all the time.
Isn't everything touched at every instant
by now?

Blossoms fall away, and new growth appears.
New growth falls away, and blossoms appear.
We walk the middle way, by night and day.

The past seems always to be right there, with the future waiting.
The past waits behind, while the future always seems beyond.
There's only always
now.

Regret cannot undo the past, and hope—hope is not change.
Hope cannot undo the past , and regret is not change.
We walk the middle way, by night and day.

So triumph fades, and failure will come.
Yet failure fades, and triumph will come.
Now changes everything,
but cannot change itself.

Time's a friend, but an enemy, too,
bringing heartache and wisdom.
Time's the magician and the illusion.

There is always only now.
We walk the middle way, by night and day.
Pushing the wave does not turn the tide.
Now

touches everything at once
teasing the eternal.
So: now.

# Rodeo

Oh, dear god, I love the changes,
but they can be so hard,
full of passion's marketplace of pain and gain.
With its symptoms and its systems
and the seasons and the reasons.
this rodeo grants every soul
free rein.

When the ties that bind are broken
and the circle gains a chair,
when the upper room has added one more band,
when the train that needs no ticket
has departed right on time,
the rodeo just finds
another hand.

Oh, dear god, I love the changes, but they can grind it fine.
Can't we follow some dirt road
in handmade shoes,
down around the curving waters
to a cabin in a clearing,
where the by and by's not traded
for a bruise?

There's a better land awaiting, oh!
But this one here is mine.
Let me pay the price myself
that I demand.
Let me grab a handy hammer
while still holding hands with time.
Let me build a little place where we can stand.

Oh, the work will be unfinished here,
that's truer than we know.
Some days the mist will pearl and track our panes.
And the quiet might be broken
by a cry that comes
too late.
We need to open up the gate and lift the chains.

So the circle isn't finished, joyous hallelujahs
hushed.
It's the silence of the stars falls on my ear,
says the better land awaiting
isn't just beyond our gate,
while these scars
can't matter much because
          we're here.

# So

The well of words was too deep for my dad.
Oh, when they'd wet his lips we'd see a smile,
but not so much, and only for a while.
Just sitting there in silence made him glad.

So, it was mainly Mom who made the song.
She'd try to put her heart into the notes,
but usually it hid among the coats.
I couldn't sit and listen very long.

I wanted more of him and less of her,
but what I wanted didn't count for much.
So. In the end, they never got in touch.
It took some deaths for greetings to occur.

Now all the paths have narrowed down to none.
The well of words has sunken past repair.
The coats don't need to act like no one's there.
A master's come to show us how to shun.

So: master how to shun what's left undone.

# Knot



My parents gave me a handmade knot
that has no ends.
It writhes, but can't be caught.
It turns upon itself and reconnects to close the loop.
So it may tangle,
braid in circles round a center it respects,
then cross itself in restless promenade.
But it's one piece, a knot I can't untie.
You're not allowed to cut it or you'll die:

that's just their rule.
They say the hardest part's just telling all the knots apart,
the ones that twist themselves around the beating hearts
of saintly folks,
say, daughters and, say, sons.

I pulled my laughter out and said their prayers,
        and when the knot was not, we went upstairs.

# Night

It seems the world grows smaller
in the night
without the light.
The clouds dismissed, horizon's on the shelf,
silhouettes dissolved
without a fight,
shadow teeth of trees,
the sky itself.

I settle for the little suns:
my chair,
a lamp's mild flare
upon a book, or flicker of TV.
Rest for now.
Light has gone to prayer.
Stumble after shadows
I can see.

My fortune's not much larger
than my hand.
A grain of sand.
Yet turn,
and see the stars from my front door.
When the moon is new
perhaps I'll understand
why the deep keeps rushing to my shore.

# Longer



Let this moment last a little longer.
I can't just slip away before we're through,
nor satisfy my promises to you,
yesterday and yesterday.
Be stronger.

There's still time for time, before the birdcalls.
The full moon's shining brighter than the dawn,
waves retreating,
beating like your footfalls.
Eternity's enraptured by my lawn.

Everything has chosen now to pause.
Better not to whisper or it's broken.
We're listening to everything unspoken.
We're basking in the dark as it withdraws.

My walls are falling, undividing tears,
stringing laughter to the times I cried.
I can hear your heart beat through my years,
cherishing our pilgrims side by side.

Everything is respite and believing.
Transient poise. The moment, moments,
leaving.

So melancholy blessed this newest day.
The dew, the dimming stars,

the empty bay.

# Green Gulch

The breezes die down.
The world resolves behind me.
One leaf pats the pond.


The grasses whisper.
Mountains separate from sky.
The breezes die down.


One leaf pats the pond.
The sky and the sun quiver.
The grasses whisper.

# Green Gulch Farm



Things I've never heard:
grave gavotte of cottonwoods
the rhythms of their sway

What I've longed to taste:
the sweetness of the valley's mist
sating appetite

Things I've never seen:
temple bell's calm resonance
silence washing back

What I've longed to feel:
my beloved's breath, this breeze
filling my embrace

Things I have savored:
bouquets of seasons' gleaning
sage's modesty

What I never knew:
this flock of waving poppies
waiting for my kiss

# Crush

I have a crush on silence.
When she's near she makes my heart relax.
I want to hear her orchestra of possibility,
where every beat awaits her composition.

Just now the wind is shushing crowds of trees to settle down.
They won't bend their knees into waiting rows of laps.
Their ability to shadow-shout and dance in one position
is a concert without clamor.
Mobility is overblown.
Each breeze is a musician.
Patiently they make the matter clear.

If I am still,
and breathe,
what will I tease?

# Summer, Green Gulch



Bushes bow down low.
Branches applaud its swift leap.
Laughing, the stream turns.

The tumbling stream chuckles,
teased by stones and shifting shade,
licking my fingers.

A sun-splashed stone,
once pressing back the current,
is held here, dripping.

# Names

the flowers all have names
like they belong to me
or daisy in a bucket
the tallest trees look down
before they fall
and claim they see it all
but none of that is true

the fern's family tree
is found in stone
but not its name
the mother of the moss that lived on that old rock
beneath the falls of that old stream before it fell
might give the rock a name
better than you
but it would not be true

there was a time
          ah let it go
there was a time when adam gave a name to everything
it didn't work
nothing can be claimed or known
because it's named
our names don't mean a thing
but if the truth sets us free
and I hear it speak to me
most likely it will call me out by name

# After

After I have seen and heard the sea
enough, declined a flirting breeze
enough, a bird nearby agrees
to be the herald of epiphany:

—Everything has changed! You were asleep!
Memories don't matter now.
Past is ashes anyhow.
Promises from yesterday don't keep.

Can you hear me?
Do you believe in me?
Am I to set your mind at ease, force the truth onto its knees
just for you?
Just so you can see?

I won't go along.
I'll sing my songs and leave.

Ask the leaves to matter and then
listen to them chatter.

Everything is
right

where it belongs—

# Enough

They said there wasn't quite enough for me.
I waited till the crowd had moved along.
I begged to disagree.
Silence left me strong.

They scatted trumpery lessons on the way.
I couldn't fathom laws beyond the noise.
Perhaps another day.
License coined new joys.

I find myself far off from the inner ring.
Whole hosts have bowed their heads to hear the prayer.
Lost secrets seem to sing.
That will be my share.

The fires are smoldering as the kinsmen sleep.
I pull my comforts closer to my breast.
Raw dreams will make the leap.
Grace will do the rest.

# Beach



This is the place where sky can meet the sea,
and sea, the beach.
And on the beach is me.
Some days the sky wells up with tears.
Some days it cries.
But then the wind will shift,
the sun will shine,
the surf will sigh, all fears dry out.
The same with me. You get my drift.
These limits: where the rules might change,
the strange begins,
and in or out may rearrange.
Humility comes swiftly on such shores.
What we hold or trust might not apply.
The unexpected comes through hidden doors.
I hold my empty hands up to the sky.
       Nothing will be lost when it is finished.
       All will be well, all will be undiminished.

# Well

She likes to watch an old guy when he's young.
She'll look around his eyes, then move her mind
and dial to strip the years and see the child.
There's always one who led him to old age,
maybe not before his heart was broken,
but, rather, breaking every day, until
familiar cracks could leave their subtle scars
within his smile, late tears behind his eyes.

        their fathers lost, the tones their mothers' tongues
        wove over babes for restless dreams to find,
        now, distant hymns,
        the quake of waking wild to unknown walls,
        the paralyzing rage blindsiding any consolation spoken,
        the shame a vagrant, gentle scold can spill into the soul,
        the single stain that mars the perfect guise,
        the very fact of lies

They could not believe
that hope and trust deceive.
Yet past the curtains of his mind
a man may mend what time unwinds.

She might see the dawn before it aches.
She might bear a mystery it takes.
And if it turns that nothing's her new guest,
well, everything will put her mind to rest.

Yet if it turns that nothing's ever lost,
then there's no need to reckon with the cost.

# Wine



She liked her scotch, but switched to wine, white wine.
Perhaps her stomach troubled her,
a sign she needed food instead of smoke and sleep,
and wine was nearly food.
She seemed so tired  from all the golfing,
book clubs, dates to keep. But if you risked a peek,
pushed her, inquired about the bills piled on her desk,
the food spoiling undisturbed, the—torpor-tude!
—Just don't see her unwashed clothes or hair!
Don't ask about her balance, rebuilt knees,
or sense the aneurysm under there.
No crosswinds for her willful glide path down,
please. So hard. Hard.
If we let her, she will go.
She wants her husband back.
Just touch and go.
What does she know?

# Hide

We'll slip away through here, avoid her glance,
act ignorant and hide.
She thinks she knows me, introduced by chance,
friends of the bride.

I know a little place where no one goes.
It should be safe and warm.
You'll be the only other one who knows.
—Ride out the storm.

It isn't that I'm frightened to be seen,
because it's true; we've met.
It's the fellow there beside her that I mean.
I mean, not yet.

I say that more and more, not yet. Someday
I'll stumble at their feet.
Loving eyes will lock, with nothing left to say.
—Won't that be sweet?

# Date



I wouldn't want to make you late,
but stay a while and see.

The sun is dipping closer to the sea.

The boats, the island over there,
are darker than before.
But set against that line you see them more.

Standing here in silence on this shore
makes everything seem rare.
It's all I know of prayer.

The line where all the light decides to flee
seems like a swinging gate.
—Now go; don't miss your date.

# Boots

Pour wine into my unwashed cup.
Old slaves of ages bathed in it.
Now ruptured graves of pharaohs
dust this lip that presses mine.
All turned to dirt.

The bells that still can ring
still ring for these,
ring for all sentient souls
that melted into seas so I can dine,
and season what is left.

Wing, fin, hoof—bring it to me!
Ancient boots and modern soles!
I'll toast the bites of nature and belief.
I'll laugh, I'll weep,
to drown the stings of grief.

I married forms,
and found I'm wed to change.
Before my genes,
inside my pulse,
upon the sacramental altar on my shelf—

—two ceramic Hopi boots,
a range of strange Oaxacan beasts,
more found and fond debris
that rang a bell inside myself—

weave graces,
practiced masters of the years,
peacemakers for the wombs and tombs,
the fears.

Our host is lighting ovens.
Ashen drapes are backlit by the fires.
Home hearths are immersed.
Nearby, the coasts creep closer,
clapping palms.

Natives brushed away like dust.
The shapes of continents adrift,
whole species cursed by answered prayers,
sincere concordant psalms.

So change remains the same,
while silence waits
 and understands,
 and opens all the gates.

Where I'm from, or where I'll go,
or why,
must sing in keys
beyond the ring of me.

Not knowing is so intimate,
so close.
I'll keep removing masks until I die

I long for innocence.
I long to be immune
from every plague I diagnose.

All will be well, she said,
all will be well.

Throw out all words.
Just listen.

     Hear the bell?

# PANNIERS

# Brays



The view from my old mind is never true.
Illusion always sends my thoughts askew,
and now the light is also failing me.
The center of my sight is turning black.
I use the corners like a spy to see
the edges, sideways, in a sneak attack.
Step unsteady, compromised by age,
ashen scent of innocence and sage.
But don't let me forget I never knew,
and don't let me revere the good old days.
I'll juggle all the answers I outgrew.
tap dance to a donkey's brightest brays.
I'll honor all the silence and the shade,
and glory in the spectacle I've made.

# Oaxaca, Presentation Day

We were watching
    for the baby dolls they offer
        to God
while we stood
    beneath the church's overarching
        bright cross.
The priest flung
    the holy water with a
        basil branch toss,
so I stepped
    behind the crowd as he approached
        with his rod.


Then the families
    crowded closer, and I turned
        to my wife
to make sure
    she'd share the blessing when it passed
        through the crowd.
As my loved one
    moved still closer, as I joined her,
        unbowed,
I felt water
    hit my shoulder, and God's grace
        miss my life.

My old shoes
    sure aren't the shiniest, my hat's
        out of whack,
and there's nothing
    that can help me if the sky
        turns to rain.
The last message
    in my bottle was too late
        for the train,
and the lesson
    for today needed a saint
        to unpack.


Did you ever
    have the feeling that you wanted
        to go,
but yet still
    you had the feeling that you wanted
        to stay?
Start to go,
    then change your mind, begin again,
        run away,
feel so broken
    you were reeling from your yes
        back to your no?

Still the choir
        continued chanting as we watched
            the calm priest
swirl his broken branch
        again around the shrine's
            holy well.
Well, we pressed
        into the families, I strained,
            almost fell,
till he flicked us
        with his balm and, lord,
            my edgy blues ceased.


Just behind me
        I felt pressure as a couple
            came late,
We all stepped away
        to let them struggle past
            in their haste.
On his hand
        he held an echo of their saviour
            he embraced
and held high,
        while praying people pled his case.
            Celebrate!

Celebrate
     our awkward timing
          and our tardy approach.
Celebrate
     the careless blessings
          of our untimely young.
Celebrate
     the intercessions
          in our alien tongue.
Celebrate
     the vagrant raindrops
          and the changes they broach.


Any gift
     I'm bearing skyward
          is in echo of your grace,
to present
     in satisfaction
          of an ancient appeal.
Though I'm grateful to be asked,
     this child will never
          be ideal.

Such an ancient race, from trees to knees.
It seems our greatest glory's commonplace.

## Blessed

So often it's a kiss that missed the heart,
a helpful bluff doubling down
on the expense of spirit lying in shame.

Betrayal changes everything,
what we know or knew or bound for our tomorrow.
What's revealed? Not what was true.

I'm not a christ by any means.
I could not foresee.
I did not agree.

Then, oh! the shocks fell.
Oh, when the shocks fall! So
hard, so hard to begin to think again.

My thoughts melted like wax.
Trust poured out like water.
Broken, unlocked, all the treasure loosed.

Rage and tears fail.
—We are met here to reason with disaster.
—It was just a trial. We can negotiate.

Yet here are our broken hearts, handed back to us,
cracked stones, puzzles growing pieces.
They will never mend the same, of course.

Should we knit honeycombs of rocks and tears,
each question always answered by the next,
our grace distilled to staunch a cataract?

Tears, turn to oil and roar back up our falls!

No, now. We've been given a great gift
on a grave occasion,
and we must tear it open, patiently.

Violence is total, in each breath.
Each breath winds down the bay to death.
Each little death can prime our souls to sail.

Surely there's a holiness in the marrow of the heart.
I would be whole again, be born again, in part,
another start for every crumbled part.

A humble path to everywhere winds through my bones
until I'm found, profoundly unalone,
no longer blind, just lost, in mystery.

For remorse, there's absolution.
She'll pardon you; that's what we often do.
You'll cast a shadow.

Hold my heart. Consider this.
Don't turn; let's not forget.
Oh, loves, oh, lives, now hear our prayer:

> Blessed be the bells that cannot be unrung,
> each lump of coal, and raven's heart, and empty bowl,
> and all the songs unsung,
>
> the hymns that lie in all the tongues, each beat, each blade
> of grass; bear fruit and multiply, then, all in good time, die.
> I will. I know the way.

## Hat in Hand
for Welly

My daughter wanted to know about the mine,
the nights I worked there, and how and why.
She'd taken a fresh interest in me,
and the me in her,
and she wanted my stories
up and down and in and around,
little lantern on a hat, walls dripping,
veins of copper green, or gold and silver,
rocks dropping, tracks and camelbacks,
and the elevators down.

What does she know? She's never been there.
So I could suddenly claim the whole damn mountain,
the dying tractor driver in the lethal mist
bulldozing the growing lake of silt flatter and wider,
and Bridal Veil Falls,
and the town, and the upper valley ranches,
and the aspen trees
and the moon and the stars.
She's wise enough
at the least
not to take my word about the moon as gospel.
(She's always open to a new point of view about stars.)
She waits for me to return to earth,
questions me toward facets
assayed more distinct and rare.

So I open up and take deep breaths
and help her poke around for treasure,
trying not to take it personally
while I'm taking it,
you know,
personally,

that part, most particularly,
about the ball bearings grinding ever finer
silt
hoping to find enough alchemy
to turn into a mountain again
or maybe
into just one aspen tree's branch
quaking across the moon
under our stars.

By God, I love this young woman for listening;
it makes me shake in my boots.

## Trifles

Well, I'm growing blind,
a little bit,
the center bit.
My hearing, it descended long ago,
        and worsens as I go.

*Just a moment.*
*Let me mourn the vision I forgot to use.*
*My hearing? Not so much.*
*Amen.*

But I don't mind,
just mind a little bit.
My weight's ascended,
and my strength
        is packing up to go.

*Can you mourn a belly that's still growing?*
*It's ever easier to touch the earth.*
*Poor me.*

So far, my blessings have been mostly kind.
We've seen enough, survived enough.
These losses are just trifles,
        trifles left behind.

*Humph.*

All this unraveling
by day, by day and through the night,
And laughter, like the hero from the deep,
traveling home at last
        to claim me in my night!

*By day I still attempt to see to weave.*

Goodbye, I'll say,
goodbye, old mind.
We've held grudges long enough.
          All sense and notions, only trifles.
Empty, broken cup.
          Patience—be so kind.

*Pour one more glass of wine.*

# Broken

We'll meet again someday.
I'll think of you, my heartaches,
as my friends,
though time has pulled apart
the bread we might have broken
in the end.

We should have known our callow dreams
would founder with such careful schemes.
We left the best
unspoken.

In that unseasoned wild,
where you tracked my vagrant profile
bending low, then tapped me on the arm,
you, you were as lost and lonely, oh!
as I.
Oh, I know.

Old friends, my prodigals,
let's reconcile.
The pass ahead
is not for angels only.

But when we meet again,
to cherish all the losses
as our grace,
remember what the cost, remember what the
cost,
to sacrifice the shameless
in our place.

Lonely scraps of right
stripped from love's skirt
could never canvas
all the naked poor,
patch ignorance,
mend hurt.

Old masters, friends,

I sacrifice my crosses.

The pass ahead's not only for the blameless.

# Innocence

Our innocence should not be underrated.
The wisdom of old age is overstated;
it doesn't spring from years of savage life,
accumulating modern toys or wealth,
nor navigating safely through the strife of love and war
while salvaging some health.
No need to flourish all your battle scars and broken hearts,
or light up fat cigars.
If a heart is breaking, share the tears.
If the storm is roiling, cherish rain.
The challenge of our souls is not our fears.
All will be lost at any cost.
What will remain?
Let innocence breach every brick and board,
and fold into our arms
till we're restored.

# Cottonseed



Yes, we coaxed her,
little  widow, new,
past trains and planes and taxi tips,
bags up crooked stairs to see the bed
we would not let her use
until night
fell.

First, down the steeply cobbled streets,
across the terrace stones to the veranda,
to our tea, to the open view below.
Ragged smiles. Comfort chamomile.
Warmth at the lip, and sighs. Almost herself
again. The unexpected
cottonseed

drifting lightly through the breeze.
Cottonseed across our shoulders
and through the trees, across the sky,
misting the late light, embracing the valley,
caressing her hair, her
breast. Oh, bless her
heart.

# Inside

At the heart of it, past pride and flaws,
innocence resides,
sheer perfection as first cause.
Then it hides.

Finding it again, past pride and flaws,
circumstance decides,
navigating chance and laws.
Bumpy rides.

Cherish ignorance and loss because
infants must. Besides,
children see what promise draws.
Age divides.

Ignorance is bliss, and without flaws.
Freedom has no sides.
Laughter climbs; the king withdraws.
Hearts are guides.

Plead your innocence, past pride and flaws.
Shorten reason's strides.
After all the answers, pause.
Taste inside.

# Spring Two



The birds are my best friends.
They let me know that they're beside me everywhere I go.
So, writing this, the pulse that never tires
is syncopated surf, soft soaring thrush,
and chitter and response of calling choirs
in sighing trees whose chambers never hush.
The company I keep sings heaven's song,
and heaven knows where an old man's words belong.
I remember once, and this was long ago,
a desert's winter night, alone at home,
starred silence belled the sky and snow below
and clarified the limits of my sight.
Oh, little man (I heard) best not to fear,
but cry your prayers for grace,
grace anywhere.

# My Rock

When my life broke in two
casually mislaid on an end table
amid the smoke, the openings
the closings
graduate schools and politics
gluttonous war
and cheap wine
famished and dirt poor
prodigal, cast away
I felt a sudden free-fall
a lifting pause that fell like silence
in the company of intimates.

My friends took pictures
and held their peace
as they watched
for the invisible to manifest
the fall-apart to grow
like a melon rolling, splitting open
on an ashy carpet.

Meanwhile,
I remained ignorant
laying mindfully
cantilevered over a valley wall
my heart holding its breath
seeping within

nectar, ichor, sap
heal and seal
this feckless vessel
so it can stand again

arms on the ropes,
boxed in the corner
and bear
some modest spray of grace.

That's when I found a rock.

"This might be my lucky rock."
I don't like to think of those days

but I love the rock
the promise it's held
through doubtful years.

A different color from the rest
deeper, pure
broken just to fit inside my grip
smooth from some distant stream
and soothing for my thumb
to rub, thoughtlessly.

Big and small enough
to carry away in my pocket
for a day.

I have it still.

# Patient

Each breath I draw is given by your leave.
Every breath's a gift I can't conceive.
It's no small thing to make a world so grand,
where every friend is different from his mate,
and every moment has a brand-new date,
and all I  know, I still can't understand.

Remembering the past from way up here,
I watch the limbs and kisses disappear.
Once in a while I stop to hear my heartbeat;
once in a while a smell recalls a road.
In someone's eyes I trace an ancient code
—the next I'm lost, and all is lost. So sweet!

So sweet the patient light
 that slips inside the least of things.
And waits.
And does not  hide

# Waters



My paddle dips and wheels my prow around.
I kneel for traction, seeking higher ground.
Perhaps my craft will not survive this trip.
What sudden cliff or gentle beach I find
would be the same approached by any ship.
The greedy deep might prove it's less than kind.
The waters play no favorites to the fast,
for everyone is reticent at last.
So I've been told. Yet on the waters roll.

The songs will sigh of love and fortune lost,
the boys will wring the wrong to save their souls,
but still the waters wave and must be crossed.

It's all a part of me:
the wave, the tide, the deep;
and you,
Beloved, you,
my guide.

# Descending

If I should want what I don't have,
billions, beaches, buildings,
I'm still poor—
deference, acclaim,
the more alone.

Cherishing the comforts of home, family, friends,
more poor,
for I've not found the rest—
libraries unread, music unheard, creatures unnoticed, planets unex-
plored,
the more unknown.

Opinions, scolds, sermons, cadence,
words unwise,
unlearned in all the tongues of service, art, and instrument—
untried, unsaid,
struck dumb.

I haven't heard the warnings,
birdsong, cries, or silence,
tuned to the familiar—
traffic, righteousness, or thunder,
ignorance revealed.

With or without possessions I am poor.
With or without desires I'm alone.
Silence shouts for calm,
and grace
is endlessly restless.

Given, never gained.
Abused, it salves.
Naked, it is modest.
It sings with silence.
Unseen, it dances.

When I rub my hands for the warmth,
I place them together.
When I have to check my footing,
I bow my head.
Awkward, for balance, I lift my palms akimbo.

Fall from grace
back into grace descending,
and every heart's beat holds my hand
and gripping—
sets me free.

# Smile

There's not a finer blessing than bathing in a smile.
When a flush of pleasure ripens, a heart spills in the eyes.
Some saints have found their virtue by gamboling awhile,
surprised to find a smile was wise.

A broken smile tells stories that trace the awkward lines
between the rock and hard place, the intimate redoubt
of longing for the sunrise, for a passage, absent signs,
so grace can stumble its way out.

So little can be treasured as worthy of the heart,
the heart that seeks the secrets transfiguring the pain.
May breaking hearts be honored, each beat refine the art
that renders smiles, though tears remain.

# Edges

The lines we scribe between things don't belong
to this or that, can't score the right from wrong.
If the scene we've built should spring a mist
and, since we're mostly water, just one drop
should just drop, a tear fall like a fist
on our account,
the world won't close up shop.
That little bird will sing its mourning hymn.
The sun will sneak beneath the widest brim.
So try to build the figures for your breath
to stir the edges
as the grasses grow
and dye each leaf with swaying shades of death.
For everything we know will have to go.
       To claim the changing world and prise each piece,
       prize the transient life and claim your peace.

# Draw

for Marguerite

Sometimes she's blue,
sometimes she's black and blue.

You'll see her livid white,
aware of every slight,
or see her peach, bruised by the bin,
but ripeness bursting from the skin,
not amber, no, but freckled gold,
and yes, moon silver, older,
rich in age,
yet green as a sage
naively setting forth
with, perhaps, a little choler,
so also red, from rage
or the sun and one two many drinks,
but then the edges pinked,
scallops of incisive care, rose hipped hope
to tame the rising slopes ahead,
tipped with a thwart of puce—don't ask!

She can be mired garden brown in daily tasks,
dirt brown, bark brown, moth umber,
humble, prone to slumber in the shade,
so here perhaps a hint of jaded roots,
worn out boots,
half-peeled orange laughing by her hand,
beneath the leaves, beside the trees, on land.
Isn't she grand?
Let her wear the purple hat. Give her a wand.
She'll wave her hand and draw a line
across the frame, right through the spine,
rend the tent, one broad stroke,

holy smoke!
She'll conjure up the great beyond
while someone peels her grapes
and everyone escapes into the blue.

Sometimes she's blue.

Sometimes she's black and blue.

Sometimes the light
will catch her just right
and you can see right through
          to you.

# Still

If I could have one token at the last
to bear with me, it wouldn't be something
I held in my hand, no, not rose or thorn.

If I could bear just one at any cost,
no book, no photograph of where I've been
or sunlight on your face or painted shore.

No, none of these. For after all that's passed,
some floorboard's creak or summer crickets, ring
of a chapel's bell—no. These could not be borne.

I savor tears, but tears are never lost.
No incense, honey, dreams, or ashes when
at last I turn to close the open door.

How could I part one snowflake from the rest?
Still, as all is changing for our guest,
I'll bear away a token in my chest.

# Now

<br>

Laughter has a way of turning round.
I share a joke, discover it's on me.
Everything I want, I've already found.
Every shadow hints at what I see.

Together, in a different world, night fell.
I couldn't close the gate or calm the dogs.
You were gone, or late; the shadows wouldn't tell.
I dropped the key beside the splintered logs.

Sometimes I've spent the night outside your door,
waiting till my shadow reappears.
Every day I've learned to love you more,
and tracked your trail of beauty through my fears.

Every night grew kinder than before,
till now we share the deep as daylight nears.

I can't forget the ordinary hour
that hides inside the ordinary day.
Sometimes it holds extraordinary power
to shove this ordinary world away.

Beside you, in this ordinary world, day broke.
Now the paper thumps outside. I find my cup
filled for me, waiting by the chair. I stroke
your hair in thanks and lift my chalice up.

Sometimes I spend my days beside the shore,
waiting till my shadow disappears.
Dear, every day I've loved you that much more,
And now I've loved you years and years and years.

# Walk

It came to me one day
when I had walked
about as far as I could go:
       my love and I live in forever now.

The little gifts upon my brow,
the disked and plowed and seeded furrows there?
My harvest.
       Share our sheaves and fruit.

A chili pepper nestles with a boot
among the tears and honeyed yams,
near Halloween,
beside a collie's smile.

Small fears are past the smoking aisle.
Avoid the rush.
Don't mention that we talked.
Stay open wide to honor thieves.

Look underneath
the budget for the leaves.
       The blood and body of the lambs
        might huddle there to host both high and low.

I walk from here to way off there.
I walk about as far as I can go.
My love and I live in forever now,
once here,
       through here, past here,
       so high and low.

# Magic

She turned old age into a magic act
and conjured from her minions what she lacked.
While evenings were spent in instead of out,
and watered wine became a drop too much,
she learned to swing doors open with a pout.
Her cards were dealt with just a cut and touch.
She left off reading books and paying bills.
She had her people organizing pills.
She'd done a lot of work. She was tired.
Blessings turned to labor, given time.
The phone, a face: numbers, names required.
Each bath was one more waterfall to climb.
She left an open face and empty hand
behind and vanished. I still don't understand.

# Stone's Roll

A tattered smile above some stone-braced sticks,
limp sleeves that summon and dismiss, with flicks
as casual as the breeze. He has no hand
to hold opinions in or close the gate,
to point a path to glory or demand
your silence so the crickets can debate.
This wisp of man conducting wind was built
to chasten birds, who prosper without guilt.
Some woman knew a man and drew his smile,
perhaps. Perhaps she offered up his shirt
to guard the green, then sat awhile, awhile.
And gathered up some stones. And traced the dirt.
A stone's roll from intention, past the plan:
the dancer and the dance, without the man.

# Plain



If I could see a thing and see it plain,
I wouldn't use my eyes,
believe the light's disguise,
to see it as it is and will remain.

The senses try, and fail, to render time.
The grain remains the same,
puts time itself to shame,
a subtle author always in his prime.

Tell me this:  The one you love, before
she sailed to you, was she
all you lived to see,
and more, and yet the same on every shore?

I've never seen the heart I've loved grow older,
however much we shared,
however deep I cared.
I've only seen the story life has told her.

# Quick

These trees,
oak and olive, pine and fir, towering eucalyptus,
instruments of wind and woodpecker,
spark and saw,

blind before the obvious
and deaf to song or shout,
things never credited
that slip away unknown.

Deep buried moments find the space
to throw their shadows, too,
standing bravely, like promises challenged,

holding up their arms in prayer and praise,
thanksgiving for these hearts
that couldn't look away, that suffered,
to the breaking,
twigs and branches,
here, and there.

Every moment fells the tree,
hooks a bit of quick,
until, finally, it only stands for how it reached.

Embraced by clay brushed at the root,
thousands of tiny kisses, leaving,
bear it away to open, ethereal mansions
of spray and scatter, scent and sky,
atom by atom.

Worn, torn, or cry-cast,
whatever quaking covenant borne
was surely kept,
proven with each downcast glance,
the layered litter, sapped veins,

witness bearing to our wake,
through every, any gate,
through silence, through the skylit dark,
to home, all in all,
as these, these trees.

# Hush

Oh, hush, hush, somebody's calling my name.
What shall I do?
There isn't much time, they say.
Oh, lord, what shall I do?

*hush on the hill and wait*

Hurry, hurry, come to the light to see.
Go to the breast.
There's honey and milk so sweet.
I'll rest a while at the breast.

*shush, be still, it's late*

Step once, twice, tumble out in the sun,
practice my dance,
I'll stumble to kingdom come
and fall down for my dance.

*rush past your grace and sprawl*

But hold, hold, my partner's finding my hand,
sharing these stars,
carousing with fierce abandon
beneath our pious stars.

*blush when you hear the call*

Now soft, soft, somebody's crying for me.
Come to my arms.
A banquet's what you need,
so, soft, come to my arms.

*lush as the evening's veil*

Count them, count—two four eight, they grow.
Where do they lead?
The points of the compass rose
won't show us where they lead.

*lush as the petals' trail*

The days, the years, range over mountains and valleys,
rise and then fall,
their fields like blooming bellies,
swelling high, and panting, fall.

*blush as you see them sprawl*

Listen, listen, every key on the piano sounds
filling our halls.
The crowds on the concourse join,
their voices filling our halls.

*rush to the front and call*

Now wait, wait. Somebody's calling my name.
What shall I do?
Near dusk of our endless day,
oh, lord, what shall I do?

*shush, be still, it's late*

Oh, hush, hush, the fruit of this perfect day,
sweet on the lips as you,
still longing for the feast,
and all of it left for you.

*hush on the hill and wait*

# Dear

I am preparing for a great sadness
and for the wake thereafter.
Some will imbibe and others will wonder.
But I will know, and I will be drunk
with awful grace.

I've waited so long
to rock my prodigal son.
Well, here I am.
(If it's not so,
yet so I've been told.)

Come sit here near the edge.
The valley lights, the evening stars are waiting.
And yes, the house is quiet.
And yes, the world is calm.
But no, the walls will fall.

Some will feel the triumph of conviction,
the nature of things,
the water in the wave. A part of me,
but I'm apart.
We'll have to make soul's sense of sorrow.

And there'll be time,
an ocean of time, whole dimensions of time.
But, now, time is
our sense most fresh.
I'm praying plain.

> Earth, hold me.
> Cloud, cover me.
> Wave, rock me.

Oh, the hummingbirds are busy.
The whooping crane is graceful
until she's not.
Well, Dear, it might be turtles,
all the way down.

> Dew, rise.
> Lips kiss.
> Flame,
> bend into flame.

# Pan

Lacrimae Rerum


Was something trapped? By the pasture fence in front
lay a galvanized steel tub from several springs ago,
lasting past this winter's snow.

Against it flapped, on the post nearby, a cord,
hanging down like silk on corn, long frayed from rubbing wind
until it couldn't bend again,

and snapped,
and released its useless grip, let the pan settle down
to go nowhere at all today, rust-tempered, like the clay.

The cord flapped, tapped to the rhythm of the wind,
ringing out, with a song and dance, the tears and joys of years
for humbled eyes and ears.

Quiet clapped
between the breaths of gust and dust, while the shadows swayed with time.
So glory came and went. Nothing gained or spent.

    The horses laughed:
    Just an old pan for water, with a hole in it.

## Stars.



When you walk to the Guest House
in the dark from dinner
there is enough light to find the steps
until the last, when you see the flat begin
but might not see to step over
the last border beam.
Be careful.

But once on the nearly level
the gentle, occasional lights
will lead you along the path
right to the gate
and the door,
if you are not attracted to the flowers.

Still,
you might miss the trees,

or be distracted by th

www.ingramcontent.com/pod-product-compliance
Lightning Source LLC
Chambersburg PA
CBHW030003010826
48973CB00009B/2648